Chris Owen started to write about Hairy Mole whilst living in a tent in the hills of Figline Valdarno, Tuscany, Italy.

After travelling through Asia and teaching in Taiwan, he now lives by the sea in sunny Hove, East Sussex.

If you'd like to contact Chris, then details are available on the Hairy Mole website:

www.hairymolethepirate.co.uk

Also by Chris Owen:

Hairy Mole
and the
Pirate
Olympics

by

Chris Owen

Hairy Mole and the Pirate Olympics

by Chris Owen
Illustrated by David Mostyn

Published by Ransom Publishing Ltd.
Radley House, 8 St. Cross Road, Winchester,
Hampshire SO23 9HX
www.ransom.co.uk

ISBN   978 184167 081 2
First published in 2013
Copyright © 2013 Ransom Publishing Ltd.

Dedications

This book is dedicated to the wonderful people of Taiwan, especially the Mighty Shane FC and Neil O' Maonaigh-Lennon – an inspirational leader who ran an amazing 105 marathons in 105 days!

A special mention to: my darling wife Nikki, my amazing little girl Isabella, my soon to be born son, Edward, and to my 90-year old grandmother Violet.

A literary mention to: Grace & Dom Patterson and to all of the good people at Ransom Publishing. Thank you for reading, editing and enjoying Hairy Mole the Pirate.

Welcome to the world little pirates: Saiari Ford, Oliver Macgregor, Molly Howard, William Marshall, Jamie Block, Joanna & Alex Bass, Iago Poma, Dalton & Dexter, Eva Seddon, Tilly Grace & Jacob Furniss, Marcia Ricca, Jasmine Lockley-Smith, Amelie Miller, Emanuel Mitchell, Charlie Perkins and Rufus & Matilda Crawford – may all your voyages be filled with health, happiness and plenty of jam.

Chris Owen

One

Much anticipation

It was the middle of a **long**, hot summer and as the sun's rays warmed rosy red apples on low-hanging trees and tickled flower petals until they were *laughing* with joy, the tiny seaside village of Littleton-on-Sea got ready for the

much anticipated,

one hundred and first,

Pirate Olympics.

At the foot of Littleton Hill, around the back of a rose-covered cottage, Mrs Bulbous Mole was busily hanging out some washing to dry in her garden.

Mrs Mole p e g g e d and hung, p e g g e d and hung, until her washing basket was completely empty.

"Well, that's everything," she said with a happy sigh.

Just then, Mrs Mole heard voices from over the fence. So she stopped what she was doing and s t r e t c h e d her ear to have a good old listen.

"I can't wait for the Pirate Olympics tomorrow," said an eager girl's voice.

"Me neither. I hope the Littleton pirates get **loads** of gold medals and we win the Pirate Olympic Cup!" said a boy in return.

"What's your favourite event?" asked the girl, who was called Sparkle.

"U r m, not sure. I think it's the Tug o' War," replied the boy, who was called Smudge.

"Oh, for me it's the Hundred Metre Pirate Bucket Boot Race," said Sparkle happily.

"Oh, me too. I like that one too," agreed Smudge.

"You can't like the Tug o' War *and* the Hundred Metres," Sparkle insisted.

"I CAN SO," cried Smudge.

Mrs Mole listened until Sparkle and Smudge's voices disappeared from her lugholes.

Then, picking up her empty washing basket, she smiled to herself and walked from her well-stocked garden into her small but comfortable kitchen, to prepare some blue mongers ready for tea.

On the tiled kitchen floor, T-towel the cat was busily washing her ten fingers and toes in readiness for some feathered friends that she had invited around for supper.

"What about you, T-towel?

What's your favourite Pirate Olympic event?"

asked Mrs Mole, as she gave
the blue mongers a good
old rinse.

   T-towel   paused
(ha ha!) and thought
for a few seconds
before answering.

   "I like any event that involves not having a
smelly-bottomed pirate sitting in my kitchen
eating my fish-finger sandwiches," T-towel
smiled , before continuing with her cleaning
regime.

   "Oh T-towel, you are a sausage," laughed
Mrs Mole, as she dried the blue mongers and
placed them on the table for chopping.

Two

Are we nearly there yet?

At that very moment, in the middle of the ocean, Mrs Mole's son, Hairy Mole, was sailing a pirate ship

left a bit   and   right a bit

on course for Kettle Island and the Pirate Olympics.

The little pirate ship had two sails and bobbed ^{up} and down,

^{up} and down,

on the clear blue water, as seagulls flew overhead and the sun warmed the wooden decking.

Hairy Mole, the captain of the little ship, stood proudly behind the wheel, listening to the sounds of the ocean and sniffing salty sea air up into his large and $uncontrollable$ nostrils.

"Are we nearly there yet, Captain?" squeaked a voice beside Hairy Mole.

The particularly high voice belonged to Mr Bogey, who was Hairy Mole's best friend and the First Mate on board the little pirate ship.

Mr Bogey was a tough old pirate who had seen many a battle and swashed many a buckle.

Mr Bogey had been in so many wars that he'd lost his left leg and now had a cricket bat instead.

This 'scratch', as Mr Bogey referred to his left leg, hadn't stopped him doing any normal

pirate duties. In fact, it made him all the more determined to be doubly rough
rough

and triply tough, just to make up for it.
tough
tough

"Almost there, Mr Bogey. We shouldn't be long now," Hairy Mole said, as he turned the wheel a little bit more to the left   and then
a little bit more to the right.

"Right you are, Skipper,"   squeaked Mr Bogey, and he walked over the wooden deck to climb a bit of rigging.

Stamp,
knock.   Stamp,
knock.   Stamp,
knock.

High up in the rigging, in the crow's nest, was a young girl pirate with exceptionally large ears. She was called Guff, and she loved being a pirate almost as much as she loved being in the crow's nest.

Guff cherished the whiff of adventure on

13

the breeze and the sounds of the sea in her over-sized lugholes. Ah yes, Guff was one happy little pirate.

Suddenly, Guff spied something and called out to Hairy Mole down on deck.

"Hairy Mole, land ahoy!" Guff shouted.

"Right you are, Guff," said Hairy Mole, as he steered the ship for land.

Mr Bogey ran across the deck and squeaked out orders to the rest of the crew.

"Crevice and Pit, climb the rigging!" Mr Bogey squeaked.

"Left!" said Pit.

"Right!" said Crevice.

Crevice and Pit, the twins, zoomed straight up the rigging and waited for further squeaky instructions.

Crevice and Pit were excellent rigging climbers, thanks to their extra-large hands.

Both of the twins were very *happy* pirates and were exceptionally *happy* about being in the Pirate Olympics.

"I can't wait for the Tug o' War!" said Pit, as he hung in the rigging.

"Me neither," said Crevice, smiling from ear to ear.

Down below, Mr Bogey squeaked out some more orders.

"Pickle, get ready to lower the mainsail," he shOuted.

"Right you are, Mr Bogey," said Pickle the Pirate, who quickly ran to the mainsail rope.

Pickle was perfect for mainsail pulling, as not only was he quite tall, he also had very

large feet – which meant that he could stand very firm as he pulled on the **heavy** rope.

Pickle was also quite a stylish pirate, and today he was wearing a rather natty waistcoat with exceptionally shiny buttons.

"All ready with the mainsail, Mr Bogey," called Pickle, as he polished his buttons for the umpteenth time that day.

As the little ship began to sail closer and closer to land, the pirates began to see lots of other pirate ships that had already docked at Kettle Island Harbour.

There were lots of flags, balloons and bunting blowing on the warm, salty breeze and children ran around on the concrete harbour walls eating pickle-dogs and wearing little skull-and-crossbones hats.

"Belch!" called out Mr Bogey.

There was no response.

"BELCH!" squeaked Mr Bogey at the top of his high-pitched voice.

From down in the galley a **stomping** and a **stamping** sound could be heard.

Then a huge pirate with a m a s s i v e nose ran up the ten steps from the galley to the deck.

"Sorry Mr Bogey, I was just having one more bowl of lovely cabbage soup," said Belch the Pirate, wiping green cabbage soup from his big, stubbled chops.

"Weigh-hey the anchor please, Belch, and we'll say no more about it," squeaked Mr Bogey, tapping his cricket-bat leg on the deck.

Belch ran to the anchor and began to weigh-hey, as all the crew commenced **pulling**
pulley things,
twisting twisty things and turning turny things,

until finally the little ship docked at the edge of Kettle Island Harbour.

Three

I smell pickle dogs!

As Hairy Mole's little ship bobbed up and down, up and down, in the harbour, the crew looked over the side at all the merry-making that was being made on the shore.

There were dancing pirates, singing pirates and running pirates everywhere, and Crevice and Pit slapped their big hands together in excitement.

There were jam stalls, grog shops and pickle-dog sellers as far as the eye could see.

There was even a bouncy pirate ship, a shrunken-head stall and a 'guess how many rubies are in the jar' game.

Guff smiled with glee and waggled her ears as she climbed down from the crow's nest and joined the rest of the crew on the deck.

"Can we lower the gang-plank, Mr Bogey?" asked Guff, eagerly wanting to test out the bouncy pirate ship.

"Yes, why n ... " began Mr Bogey.

"Waaaaaaaaiiittt!"

yelled Hairy Mole, just as Pickle was about to lower the gang-plank.

Everyone stopped what they were doing and listened to Captain Hairy Mole.

"There are some very important things you should know before we go ashore." Hairy Mole scratched an itch on his bottom, before sitting down on the wooden deck.

The crew all sat down in front of him and waited to hear what important things he had to say.

"Now," Hairy Mole began, "the **Pirate Olympics** are good fun and we've all trained **very** hard."

The crew nodded and heartily agreed, rubbing their aching muscles – that they'd been exercising for at least the best part of two weeks.

"**But** there's **one** thing that you have to remember." Hairy Mole stroked his badger-rough chin.

"Don't eat a pickle-dog without chewing it?" squeaked Mr Bogey.

"Don't go ashore without lowering the gang-plank?" asked Crevice and Pit together.

"Don't do a p ... " Belch began.

"Listen!" said Hairy Mole.

The crew listened and Guff waggled her ears with extra focus.

"As long as you do your best, then I will be **very** proud of you!" Hairy Mole smiled a big gap-toothed grin.

"Now, let's get that gang-plank down – and last one to eat a pickle-dog smells like rotten turnips!"

For the rest of the day, Hairy Mole and the Littleton pirates walked around Kettle Island, ate lots of pickle-dogs, bounced on bouncy pirate ships and drank lots of grog.

After a jolly good bit of exploring, the pirates came across a **magnificent** arena that was as tall as three giraffes and as wide as twenty-nine elephants.

"This must be where the games take place," said Guff in wonder.

"Can we go in?" asked Crevice, as he edged towards the arena entrance.

"No you cannot!" said a beefy-looking guard who had been hiding behind a green wheely bin.

"Oh, I just wanted a peek," said Crevice rather disappointedly.

"A peek!" exclaimed the guard in astonishment.

"Imagine if everyone just had a 'peek', then

where would we be?" The guard shook his head.

"Well, could we just have a glimpse?" asked Hairy Mole.

"No peeks and no glimpses! Read the sign!"

The Littleton pirates all gathered around the sign and forgot all about peeking and glimpsing for a few moments at least.

"So," laughed Guff, "what are the other teams like? **The Daisy Headhunters** sound a bit wimpy and **The Pirate Pensioners** must be far too old!"

"Don't write off the Pensioners, Guff. They're so rough and tough that they could light their pipes, dunk their biscuits *and* sink a

Welcome to the
One Hundred and First Pirate Olympics

Starting tomorrow at twelve o' clock sharpish

(No peeking or glimpsing)

List of Events
• Walking the Plank • The Barrel Push
• Jumping the Nearly Dead Man's Chest
• Crow's Nest Challenge • Tug o' War
• One Hundred Metre Pirate Bucket Boot Race

Pirate Teams
• The Pirate Pensioners • The Littleton Pirates
• The Whiskers Gang • The Daisy Headhunters

Scoring
Gold = 3 points
Silver = 2 points
Bronze = 1 point
4th place = A big fat zero

Sponsored by Badger's Burp Brewery

sailor's ship **before** you've had a chance to say 'Where are my slippers?'!" Belch said, before biting into a spicy bagel that was dripping with beetles.

"Yeah, but The Daisy Headhunters, they <u>must</u> be easy to beat, right?" Guff laughed, before turning around to see the serious look on Mr Bogey's face.

"There's something you should know about The Daisy Headhunters," squeaked Mr Bogey.

"What?" quivered Guff.

"Have you heard of the **Kraken of Wintersbottom?"**

"Urm, urp, yes," gulped Guff.

"I heard the **Kraken of Wintersbottom** ate The Daisy Headhunter's captain, **Wee Gladys the Mad,**" said Pickle.

"No. It was the other way round!" squeaked Mr Bogey.

"Oh, urp," gulped Pickle and Guff together.

"And, and, and ... " stammered the twins, "what about **The Whiskers Gang?**"

"The Whiskers Gang ... " Hairy Mole began,

" ... are right behind you!"

said a **horrible,** *gravelly* voice.

Hairy Mole turned round and found himself face-to-face with a fearsome-looking pirate.

The pirate had the **darkest** eyes you have ever seen and wrinkled skin that looked as **thick** as a rhino's bottom.

"I'll wager you're still as wet behind the ears as a cabbage on a compost heap!" **growled** the pirate, as he *tweaked* Hairy Mole's cheek with a pinch that could have crushed a humbug.

"Good to see you again, Bill," Hairy Mole lied, as his cheek began to **throb**.

Captain Bill Whiskers, the Captain of **The Whiskers Gang**, stroked his **long** grey beard and smiled through his gold-toothed mouth.

"I wish I could say the same about you, Hairy Boil," laughed Captain Whiskers, with a laugh that could make a puppy cry.

"So these are your crew then, are they?" Captain Whiskers looked at Hairy Mole's crew and **growled** a horrible tuna-breath **growl**.

"Yes they are," said Hairy Mole, proudly puffing out his chest.

"Well then, now I'm even **more** certain that my gang is going to **win** the Pirate Olympic Cup!" Captain Whiskers laughed, before turning around to leave.

1, 2, 3, 4 ...

Hairy Mole clenched his fists and counted to ten.

"Oh – and one more thing," said Captain Whiskers.

" ... Eight, nine, what?" said Hairy Mole through gritted teeth.

Captain Whiskers pointed to a grog stall where two of the **biggest** and **baddest** pirates that you've ever seen were **whacking** each other on the head, just for fun.

"Whoever is doing the Tug o' War may want to say hello to my boys Barry and Billy over there."

Crevice and Pit gulped and their knees began to knock together, as Barry and Billy Whiskers began to **stamp** on each other's feet, just because they liked it.

"Urm, I think it's time we went back to the ship," said Hairy Mole quietly. "We're going to need **lots** of cabbage soup and an early night if we're going to be ready for tomorrow."

With that, Hairy Mole and his crew walked back to their little ship and had **extra** helpings of steaming green cabbage soup, before retiring to their hammocks for a good night's kippage, to be right ready for the Pirate Olympics that would be starting the very next day at **twelve o'clock sharpish**.

Four

Cutlasses polished

The next morning the sun was shining down on Kettle Island and the scent of pickle-dogs and turnips filled the air.

After much scratching and parping and *picking* and *flicking*, Hairy Mole and his crew walked up the ten steps from the galley to the deck and stood stretching their limbs in readiness for the one hundred and first Pirate Olympics.

The crew were wearing special pirate vests, extra-baggy shorts and super-smelly socks that could stand up on their own.

"It's a good day to win some medals, Mr Bogey," said Hairy Mole, as he raised his warty hands into the air.

"It certainly is, Hairy Mole," Mr Bogey agreed, bending down to touch the end of his cricket bat leg and letting out a little parp in the process.

"What's the first event?" squeaked Mr Bogey, as they walked down the gang-plank and onto the concrete harbour wall.

"It's the Walking the Plank event," said Guff, as she kicked a little stone off the harbour wall and into the water below, just so she could enjoy the plipping sound.

"That's Pickle's event!" squeaked Mr Bogey.

"It certainly is," said Pickle and he took out a freshly polished silver cutlass that shimmered in the sunlight.

"And what time does it start?" asked Mr Bogey.

"TWELVE O' CLOCK SHARPISH!"

yelled all of the pirates together.

When Hairy Mole and the crew got to Kettle Island Arena, it was **packed** with pirates all *cheering* and **grow**ling and *gnashing* and *snarling*. There were smelly pirates, **dirty** pirates and pirates who looked like they hadn't eaten any vegetables for weeks.

"What a great atmosphere," said Guff rather nervously.

"It makes you proud to be a pirate," smiled Belch, holding a quart of grog in his hand.

After some pushing, shoving and general merry-making, Hairy Mole and his crew found six seats together in the stands. Guff looked at her Pirate Olympics' programme and read out the rules for the Walking the Plank event.

"The **Walking the Plank** event is traditionally always the first event at the Pirate Olympics. It involves a plank high up above a small barrel of freezing cold and extremely dirty water.

"Pirates have to climb up a ladder, onto the plank, and force a waiting landlubber to jump off into the barrel below."

34

"Oh good!" squeaked Mr Bogey.

"Marks are awarded for cutlass
style, forced jump of the landlubber
and for facial expression and battle
cry.

Oh yes, and the pirate only
gets **three** minutes to make the
landlubber jump, or else he gets no
points at all." Everybody clapped as Guff
finished her speech.

"Good speech, Guff. Now, quiet
everybody – they're about to start!" hushed
Hairy Mole, as Belch let out a little pop.

Down below the stands, in the centre of
Kettle Island Arena, an official was officially
giving instructions to the first contestant of the
Walking the Plank event.

"Now remember," the official began,
"no climbing until I blow this whi ... "

The first contestant, Bernard Green Beard from **The Daisy Headhunters,** was no bigger than a marmot, but he was **fiercer** than a honey badger with a headache – and he didn't wait for any more official chit-chat.

"Peeeeeeeeep!"

whistled the official, even though Bernard was already half-way up the ladder.

High up above on the plank, the landlubber, Peter Parhoon, was nervously waiting with knocking knees and chattering teeth.

"Grrrrrrrrrr," growled Green Beard,

as he climbed the last rung of the ladder and stepped onto the plank.

"Urp," gulped Peter the landlubber,

as he began to back away from the tiny yet **ferocious** pirate.

"**Arghhhhhh**," yelled Green Beard, as he ran towards Peter Parhoon, swinging his cutlass around like the blades of a lawn mower.

The crowd watched and **cheered** with delight as, after much **growling** and good cutlass work, Bernard Green Beard of **The Daisy Headhunters** made Peter Parhoon, the landlubber, jump off the plank and down,

down,

down

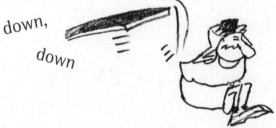

into the stinky, **freezing** cold water below.

"Gosh, that was a good one," said Pickle to Mr Bogey, as they stood at the side of the arena and waited for Pickle's turn.

A judge appeared in the middle of the arena and held up a score card with the number **8** on it.

"So, eight points to beat then, Pickle. You can do it!"

squeaked Mr Bogey, before he went through some last-minute checks.

"Cutlass polished?"

"Check."

"Boots waxed?"

"I'm not wearing boots!"

"OK, grimace and battle yell at the ready?"

"CHEEEERRRRRRRCK!"
grimaced and yelled Pickle.

"Good luck Pickle," Mr Bogey squeaked.

Pickle stood at the foot of the tall ladder and placed his cutlass in his mouth, flat side in, and began to climb up to the plank.

On the plank, the landlubber stood in front of him looking slightly cocky. He was dressed in comical pantaloons and a T-shirt that said

'I survived the plank at the 2008 Pirate Olympics'.

"Well you're not going to survive **this** plank" Pickle mumbled through his cutlass-filled mouth.

"**What?**" shouted the landlubber, with one eye on the ticking clock.

"**I said,**" said Pickle, removing the cutlass from his mouth,

"Aaarrgggghhhh!"

"Oh," replied the landlubber, but it was too late as Pickle the Pirate from Littleton-on-Sea ran down the plank, SWOOping and SWIping like an attacking crow.

"That's got him!" smiled Hairy Mole, as he watched the landlubber tumble over the end of the plank.

"Yaaaaaaaaay" cheered the Kettle Island Arena.

"Come on Littleton!" shouted Belch.

"The judges are going to give their decision," whispered Mr Bogey.

The crowd watched as the judge walked to the centre of the arena and waited for silence, before holding up a card with 8.5 on it.

"Yaaaaay," screamed Guff. "We're in the lead!"

Crevice and Pit looked through the 'Pirate Olympics' programme, as the crowd waited impatiently for the next contestant.

"It says here that the next contestant is from **The Whiskers Gang** and her name is Pirate Betsy."

"Who's Pirate Betsy?" the twins asked Hairy Mole.

"She's the kind of pirate who will **drive a cutlass through your heart** and sing you a song about turnips at the same time," said Hairy Mole, as he watched Pirate Betsy climb the tall ladder, lift her cutlass into the air and charge down the plank.

High up on the plank Pirate Betsy, the daughter of Captain Whiskers, tossed her cutlass from hand to hand and unleashed a scream that would have struck fear into the caverns of Mount Jahebas.

"Eeeebliiiiiiieeekkkk!"

screamed Pirate Betsy.

Without even a *prod* or a *poke*, the landlubber turned tail and ran to the end of the plank.

Pirate Betsy's red and white petticoats ballOOned under her black frock, as she chased down her prey.

A *flash* of silver glinted in the midday sun as the landlubber leapt to safety with a perfectly sliced B on his shirt and an equally impressive look of fear upon his face.

"That's a sure-fire gold medal if ever I saw one," said Mr Bogey.

The crowd waited as the judge walked to

the centre of the arena, lifted up his score card and revealed a big fat number 10!

There was a huge round of applause from the crowd.

The final contestant was a *swarthy-looking* Pirate Pensioner who had an eye-patch and seven earrings in each ear. He hobbled and cobbled up to the tall ladder, before asking for assistance to reach the first rung.

The impatient crowd watched as the pirate, who was called Lightning Jack, s l o w l y climbed the ladder and got to the top, before pausing for a nice sit down and a rest.

The landlubber waited cautiously, with one eye on the t i c k i n g clock, but just as he was thinking that this was the easiest job he'd ever had, there was an **almighty roar** as the Pirate Pensioner hobbled towards him, **shouting** the naughtiest words that he'd ever heard.

The landlubber was so shocked at what he heard that he toppled over backwards and down,
                    down,
                                down
into the filthy, **dirty** water below.

The judge skipped into the arena and held up the score card for the final contestant in the **Walking the Plank** event. It had a cheeky number **7** on it.

"Yaaaay!" yelled Guff. "We've got a **silver** medal! That's **two** points!"

"Yes," said Hairy Mole to himself, "but **The Whiskers Gang** have got a **gold** medal and that's **three** points."

The crowd all growled and *roared* their approval, as Captain Whiskers and his gang ran around the Kettle Island Arena carrying Pirate Betsy on their shoulders.

"Come on, let's go and say 'Well done' to Pickle," said Hairy Mole, as he *shoved* his way down the arena steps.

"The next event will be at one o'clock sharpish!"called out a loudspeaker.

"What is the next event?" asked Mr Bogey.

"That would be the Jumping the Nearly Dead Man's Chest event," said Hairy Mole.

"And who's doing that event for us, then?" squeaked the First Mate.

"Urrm, that would be you," said Hairy Mole, nudging Mr Bogey in the ribs.

"Oh is it?" squeaked Mr Bogey. "I'd better go and oil my leg!"

Five

Yo ho ho,
look at that dead man go!

With the first event out of the way, Hairy Mole decided to buy everyone a quart of grog to say **'Well done'** to Pickle for his **silver** medal.

The crowd at the **Badger's Burp Brewery** tent was particularly *rough* and *tough*, but Hairy Mole fought his way to the front and managed to get the celebratory booze without too much commotion.

Just as he was heading back into the arena, Hairy Mole felt a **tap** on his shoulder.

"Hello Hairy Mole, long time no see," said a voice that sounded like butterfly's wings dipped in honey.

"Oh yes, urrm, hello Betsy. You're looking well," Hairy Mole s t a m m e r e d , almost dropping the grog on the ground.

"I hear you've met Pa already," smiled Betsy, with a twinkle in her emerald-green eyes.

"Yes, he's lost none of his charm."

Hairy Mole looked around nervously.

"What event are you in? I'll keep an eye out for you," Pirate Betsy asked, flicking her long black hair.

"I'm in the last event, **the One Hundred Metres Pirate Bucket Boot race**," Hairy Mole said, puffing out his chest.

47

"Oh, I can just picture you in those massive boots, Hairy Mole. I hope you've shined your buckles,"

Betsy smiled.

"BETSY!"

Before Hairy Mole had a chance to blush, a *roar* came from behind the grog tent and Pirate Betsy winked at Hairy Mole, before turning around and disappearing into the crowd.

Hairy Mole didn't wait to see if Captain Whiskers was far behind. He hurried back into the arena and up the steps to give the crew their grog without further ado.

"Now, for your information,"

said Guff, as Hairy Mole's smelly bottom squeezed down beside her, "the Jumping the Nearly Dead Man's Chest event is one of the oldest events in the Pirate Olympics."

"Ffffffffffffffmmmmm!"

Belch parped happily to himself.

Guff continued,

"The rules are quite simple: once **the nearly dead man** has escaped from his chest, and his feet have touched the ground,

the pirate competitor is allowed to leap

over the chest and try to catch the fleeing, bony body."

"Sounds like fun," said Pickle, as he polished his shiny new **silver medal**.

"That's **not** the only thing," said Guff. "Once the pirate has caught **the nearly dead man**, he has to **manhandle** him back into the chest in the quickest time possible, until the lock is finally **clamped shut.**"

The crew all nodded and smiled, before tucking into their grog and settling back into their seats, as the first contestant entered the arena.

The first contestant, Mr Morris from **The Pirate Pensioners**, walked to **the nearly dead man's chest** in the centre of the arena, spat on the ground and **waited** with his hands on his hips.

A judge stood next to Mr Morris with a whistle in his mouth.

"**Peeeeeeeeep!**" the whistle blew.

All eyes were on **the nearly dead man's chest.**

"That's the beauty of this event, as you never know when the nearly dead man will actually appear," said Hairy Mole to Guff.

"Sometimes you have to wait for days,"
he chuckled quietly.

"THERE HE GOES!" yelled Guff,

as a **skinny**, nearly dead man opened the chest and bolted across the arena.

Mr Morris was ready for him, and as soon as **the nearly dead man's** rotten foot had touched the ground he leapt over the chest like a fawn in the forest.

The nearly dead man ran across the arena, dodging left and right as the crowd **shouted** and **cheered** and the seconds ticked by.

Mr Morris *threw* himself through the air and **grabbed** the **nearly dead man** around the ankle with a fixed grip.

"Oh, he's got *him*,"
said Guff rather disappointedly.

The crowd **screamed** and *yelled* as the seconds ticked away and Mr Morris ran with the struggling **nearly dead man**'s body back to the chest.

Ker chunk!

The chest was bolted and Mr Morris of **The Pirate Pensioners** waved to the crowd.

It was only then that he noticed that he was still holding onto **the nearly dead man's foot** and that the clock hadn't stopped ticking.

Quickly, Mr Morris reopened the chest and **threw** in the mouldy old foot.

"Time stopped at 40 seconds," announced the judge.

"What a load of poop," yelled Mr Morris, as he stomped out of the arena.

The next contestant, Pirate Jess from The Daisy Headhunters, had an **awful** time trying to leap her chest and was eventually given a **100 second penalty** for climbing instead of jumping.

After this terrible display by Pirate Jess, it was Mr Bogey's turn. He got up from his seat and walked down the wooden steps.

Stamp,
knock

Stamp,
knock

Stamp,
knock.

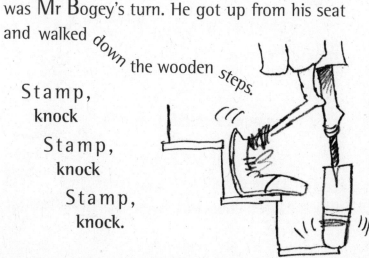

Mr Bogey walked to the centre of the arena, stood next to the chest and waited for the judge to blow the whistle.

"Peeeeeeeeeeeep!"

There was a hushed silence as everyone waited.

'Creeeeeeeeeeeeak.'

The chest opened and out flew a rotting definitely dead man with no head.

The headless corpse ran from the chest and sprinted in a straight line across the field.

The seconds started to tick by.

Mr Bogey didn't stop to think and jumped over the open chest but, as he was in mid-jump, he heard a voice **shouting** from inside the old wooden chest.

"Oi, pirate, leave my body alone!" screamed the head of the definitely dead man.

Mr Bogey lost his footing and fell to the ground in surprise.

"10, 11, 12," shouted the crowd, as the seconds ticked on.

"Get up, get up," yelled Belch.

"Come on, Mr Bogey," shouted Crevice and Pit.

Mr Bogey watched the **definitely dead man**'s body running away and, quick as a **flash**, he got to his feet and began to run after him.

Running as **fast** as he could, Mr Bogey forgot all about his cricket-bat leg, but try as he might he couldn't help running in a curve, like a banana.

As luck would have it, the **definitely dead man**'s body had **no idea** where it was running, and it ran **directly** into Mr Bogey's o u t s t r e t c h e d arms.

Mr Bogey leapt like a mongoose and caught hold of the **definitely dead man**'s waist *just* before he reached the edge of the arena.

"30, 31, 32 ... " shouted the crowd, as Mr Bogey picked up the body and raced back to the open chest.

Just as Mr Bogey was almost at the open chest, the **definitely dead man**'s head bounced out and onto the ground.

"35, 36, 37 ... "

"Look," squeaked Mr Bogey to the head, as he ran with the body under his arm, "if you bounce back in I'll make sure you get buried at sea!"

"I hate the sea!" shouted the head.

"38, 39, 40 ... "

Those were the last words that came from the **definitely dead man**'s mouth as Mr Bogey *swiped* his cricket-bat leg under the **dead man**'s chin and sent him flying back into the chest.

Ker chunk!

Mr Bogey slammed the chest shut and fell to the ground as he tried to get his breath back.

"Time stopped at 41 seconds," announced the judge.

"Yaaaaay!" roared the crowd in approval.

Mr Bogey walked back across the arena to join the crew in the stands.

Stamp, knock Stamp, knock Stamp, knock.

"Unlucky, Mr Bogey. Just one second behind The Pirate Pensioners," said Guff.

"I know, he was a slippery little **definitely** dead customer," squeaked Mr Bogey.

"At least you knocked him for six," smiled Belch, **grabbing** Mr Bogey *roughly* by the shoulders and hugging him until he let out a little trump.

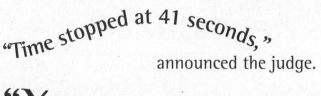

58

"Well said, Belch!" smiled Hairy Mole.

"It's just **The Whiskers Gang** left to go and we're guaranteed at least a **bronze medal**," said Guff excitedly.

"There's the final contestant, Dangerous Dan Whiskers," whispered Pickle.

"If I was a nearly dead man I'd be staying put in my chest if I knew that Dangerous Dan Whiskers was outside," whispered Crevice to Pit.

Dangerous Dan Whiskers **growled** menacingly as he walked across to the chest in the centre of the arena.

"Peeeeeeeeeeeeeeep!"
the whistle blew.

Almost **immediately** the **nearly dead man** bolted from his chest, but equally quick off the mark was Dan Whiskers, who sprung at the **nearly dead man** and **grabbed** him around the neck before he had even touched the ground.

Dan Whiskers **slammed** the lid of the chest shut and raised his hands in the air.

"Time stopped at 2 seconds,"

announced the judge.

"That's incredible! It must be a **Pirate Olympic record,"** sighed Hairy Mole.

"Hang on, there's a judges' inquiry. Something has been said by one of the officials," Pickle noticed.

Everyone in the crowd held their breath

as an **official** walked over to the centre of the arena, *whispered* in the judge's ear and handed him a little leather-bound **rule book.**

The judge nodded, turned to the crowd and read from the book.

"In the rules of 'Jumping the Nearly Dead Man's Chest', Rule 3.2, sub section 6, states that the nearly dead man must touch the ground first before the pirate is allowed to jump over the chest."

The crowd gasped.

"Gaaaaaassssssssp!"

The judge continued.

"Dangerous Dan Whiskers didn't wait for any part of the nearly dead man to touch the ground before he gripped it around the neck and shoved it back into the chest."

The crowd growled.

"Grrrrrrrrrrrrrrr!"

"Therefore, the winner of the **gold medal** of **Jumping the Nearly Dead Man's Chest** goes to Mr Morris of **The Pirate Pensioners**, with Littleton in **second place** and The Daisy Headhunters in the **bronze medal** position!"

The judge and the official were surrounded by Captain Whiskers and the rest of **The Whiskers Gang,** who were a shovin' and a shoutin' and a causin' all kinds of a din.

"Come on everyone, apart from Belch, let's get some pickle-dogs to celebrate!" shouted Hairy Mole with glee.

"Hey, why not me?" moaned Belch.

"Because, Belch old boy," squeaked Mr Bogey,

"it's your event next!"

Six

Ever so exciting!

Back home in **Littleton-on-Sea** there were all kinds of celebrations going on, as people listened on radios and watched on TV screens.

The cobbled streets were festooned in bunting, balloons and banners, and children were skipping and jumping like they'd eaten a whole year's worth of burping beans.

In the little cottage at the bottom of **Littleton Hill**, Mrs Bulbous Mole had been joined by her sister Humongous.

They sat happily together drinking tea and eating specially-made Pirate Olympic cake.

"Oh Bulbous, isn't this exciting?" said Auntie Humongous through a mouthful of chocolate-covered sponge.

"Oh yes Humongous, I'm so excited that I could burst like a balloon filled with custard."

Bulbous Mole laughed, as she poured another cup of tea for herself and her sister.

"How about you, T-towel, are you excited too?"

Bulbous Mole asked T-towel the cat, who was sitting on a **comfy** cushion, picking feathers from her claws.

T-towel licked her lips, yawned and arched her back, before turning around three times and positioning herself back onto the **comfortable** cushion.

"Oh T-towel," laughed Bulbous Mole, "you are a monger fish and no mistaking."

T-towel raised an eyebrow, closed her eyes and instantly began to dream of freshly-caught salmon, as the Mole sisters prepared themselves for the next exciting event in the Pirate Olympics: **the Barrel Push.**

Seven

Roll out the barrel
– but watch out for fishwives!

Back on **Kettle Island,** **H**airy **M**ole and the rest of t**he** **Littleton** pirates finished their pickle-dogs and joined the crowds which had started to form around the bottom of **Kettle Island Hill.**

"How are you feeling, **B**elch?" **H**airy **M**ole asked, as **B**elch limbered up for the **Barrel Rolling** event.

"Never better," said **B**elch, as he cracked his fingers together and burped to show that he'd never felt better.

"Craaaaaccckk.

Buuuuuurrrp!"

66

"Good lad! Just remember to push, not pull!" squeaked Mr Bogey.

"Will do," said Belch, as he made his way to the starting line.

"Come on, Guff," said Crevice and Pit together.

"What are the rules?"

"OK, OK," said Guff, and she cleared her throat before reading from her programme.

"Ahem. Contestants have to run to a **large** Badger's Burp Brewery cart, grab a barrel of finest quality **Badger's Burp Ale** and then *push* the barrel up Kettle Island Hill and over the finishing line at the top."

"That sounds pretty easy!" said Pickle, as he crunched into a beetle burger.

"Hmm yes, but there's one other problem," laughed Guff.

"Fish wives are placed up the hill and will be throwing an assortment of stinky fish at the contestants!"

"Uughghhghh!"

squealed the twins, as the bell sounded and the race began.

Ding a ling a ling a ling a ling!

"Go on, Belch," yelled Pickle.

As soon as Belch heard the bell, he was off and running as fast as he could. He quickly found himself in front of the other pirates.

'Come on Belch, you can do it', he said to himself, as he

got closer to the Badger's Burp Brewery cart.

All of a sudden the ground disappeared from under him as he fell to the floor and landed on his **nose**.

Belch looked up to see the bony figure of Pirate Stan from **The Pirate Pensioners** running off towards the cart.

"That old pirate biddy tripped me up!" Belch hollered.

Belch got to his feet and **ran** after the other pirates, as they were **heaving** their barrels of Badger's Burp Brewery ale from the **large** wooden cart.

Just before Belch reached the cart, Slippery Pete from **The Daisy Headhunters grabbed** a barrel but lost his footing under the weight, causing it to fall on his head and **squash** him into the ground.

Belch quickly delivered a *swift* kick to the ankles of Pirate Stan, who had just lifted his barrel on to his bony shoulders.

"Arrrgh – me ankle!"

screamed Pirate Stan, hopping about on his bony old leg.

Belch didn't stop to check on the elderly pirate's welfare.

He just scooped up his own barrel and ran towards Kettle Island Hill, leaving Slippery Pete and Pirate Stan behind.

'That's two down and one to go,'

thought Belch, as he chased after Growling Mike from The Whiskers Gang, who had already started to roll his barrel up Kettle Island Hill.

Belch and Growling Mike were neck and neck as they neared the top of the hill.

There were **fishes flying** about all over the place, and both pirates shut their eyes as rotten fish juice streamed down their faces and up their nostrils.

Suddenly, from back down the hill, there was an almighty **roar** as Slippery Pete from **The Daisy Headhunters** jumped on top of his barrel and kicked his little legs, making the barrel fly up the hill at a very fast speed.

Slippery Pete was so small and *fast* that he managed to duck out of the way of the throwing fish wives, past Belch, past Growling Mike and over the finishing line.

"**Yeeeeeeeessssssss!!**" screamed Wee Gladys the Mad and the rest of **The Daisy Headhunters.**

SLAP!

Another fish caught Belch in the face as he dived for the finishing line in third place, just behind Growling Mike and Slippery Pete.

"**Ohhhhhhhhhh!**" yelled Hairy Mole and the crew, as they watched Belch lying on the ground with a kipper hanging out of his mouth.

After much talk of 'that's supper sorted then', Hairy Mole, Belch and the rest of the crew made their way from **Kettle Island Hill** back to the arena.

"Can I have my pickle-dog now?" asked Belch, still with a bit of fish slime around his chops and a **bronze medal** bouncing on his barrel-like chest.

"I didn't think you'd be hungry," squeaked Mr Bogey.

"I'm saving this one for later," smiled Belch, showing the big fish that he'd put into his pocket.

Outside the arena another large poster had been displayed, showing the medals table.

Hairy Mole and his crew crowded around the poster and congratulated themselves for being in **joint first place** at the half-way stage.

"We just need to keep ahead of **The Whiskers Gang!**" squeaked Mr Bogey.

MEDALS TABLE

1st place
The Daisy Headhunters
2 x Bronze and 1 x Gold – 5 points

1st place
The Whiskers Gang
1 x Gold and 1 x Silver – 5 points

1st place
The Littleton Pirates
2 x Silver 1 x Bronze – 5 points

Not 1st place
The Pirate Pensioners
1 x Gold – 3 points

Sponsored by Badger's Burp Brewery

Just then, he felt a nip on his right ankle.

"Ouch!" squealed Mr Bogey in surprise.

"Don't forget about us!" screeched a terrifying voice.

"Who said that?" squeaked Mr Bogey.

"Oi, down 'ere!" yelled the horrific voice again.

Mr Bogey looked down and saw the most frightening pirate known to man or beast, Wee Gladys the Mad, the Captain of The Daisy Headhunters.

She was half the size of Mr Bogey's cricket-bat leg, but with her **fiery red hair** and crooked beak of a nose she looked more than capable of knocking **anyone** for six.

"**Urp**," gulped Guff, "Is she doing the Crow's Nest Challenge?"

"**Urmm**, don't worry Guff, just do your best and you'll be **fine**." Hairy Mole tried not to look too frightened as he followed Guff into the arena.

Then they found their seats and got ready for the next event that was due to start at **three o' clock sharpish**.

Eight

Black feathers and pointy sticks

In the centre of **Kettle Island Arena,** four **large** masts had been erected, with a crow's nest at the top of each one.

Circling above the nests were some *mean-looking* crows with beady yellow eyes and sharpened beaks, ready for **pecking** pirate heads in the Crow's Nest Challenge.

Guff ran to pick up the Littleton **pirate flag,** before running to the centre of the arena where the four masts were waiting to be shimmied up.

In the stands, Crevice and Pit were eagerly looking for the rules to the **Crow's Nest Challenge.**

"Well boys," said Hairy Mole. "Quite simply, each contestant must shimmy up the mast and hoist their pirate flag from the crow's nest.

"Then they have to slide back down and ring a bell at the bottom of their mast.

First one to **ring their bell** is the winner."

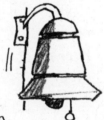

"Oh Guff will be bound to win, she's a **sensational** shimmier,"

interrupted Belch, with a mouthful of hedgehog hoagie.

Hairy Mole continued, "The only *slight* trouble is that they have to fight several

pecky crows who have decided that it's their nest and who are **not** going to let any pirates have it!"

"**Oh**, that might be a **bit** tricky then, as Guff isn't much of a fighter, **especially** not with animals." Belch finished his hoagie and **burped** like a cow.

"Buuurrrpppmooooo!"

Under her mast, Guff looked across to her **three** opponents and watched them prepare.

Wee Gladys the Mad was **grinding** her teeth and *stamping* her feet like a **wild** Shetland pony.

Fillet of Fish Fred from **The Pirate Pensioners** was smoking his pipe and reading a book about allotments.

79

And Barney Whiskers was carving his name into the foot of his mast with a **very sharp-looking** knife.

"On your marks ... "

"Get set ... " **"Go!"**

With a flap of her ears, Guff ran towards her mast and gripped hold of the polished wood between her gloved hands.

"How's she doing, how's she doing?" cried Crevice and Pit from high up in the stands.

"I think she's in third place behind Barney Whiskers and Wee Gladys the Mad," shouted Hairy Mole, as he looked through his telescope.

"Come on Guff," shouted Belch.

High up on the mast, Guff could feel her grip begin to loosen as she tried with all her might to hold onto the shiny wooden pole.

"Oh no, she's slipping!" yelled Hairy Mole, as he watched Guff slowly start to slide back down her mast.

"Hold on, Guff!" shouted Crevice and Pit together.

"Hang on, she's taking off her gloves," shouted Hairy Mole. Just then, the crowd began to cheer wildly as Barney Whiskers reached his crow's nest in **first place**.

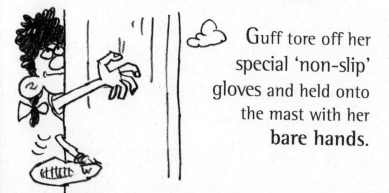

Guff tore off her special 'non-slip' gloves and held onto the mast with her **bare hands**.

She quickly looked across at the other masts and saw the *mean-looking* crows starting to circle and peck at Barney Whiskers.

"Barney Whiskers is in **first place** and Wee Gladys the Mad has just reached her crow's nest in **second place!**" Hairy Mole yelled.

Guff quickly began to inch her way up the mast, until finally she was at her crow's nest.

Guff peered over the edge and faced **three** of the *fiercest-looking* crows that she had ever seen.

"Get away from our nest!" the crows shouted angrily.

Guff ducked her head out of the way of a *sharp-looking* beak.

"Urrm, I was wondering …"

she asked politely. The crows stopped their pecking and squarking and cocked their heads onto their shoulders.

They weren't used to being spoken to so nicely.

"**Arrrrrrrrrrrghhhhh!**"

screamed Fillet of Fish Fred of **The Pirate Pensioners**, as a crow scratched at his face. Guff watched as the elderly pirate clung on to the outside of his crow's nest.

Wee Gladys the Mad and Barney Whiskers were slashing and stabbing, but the crows were protecting their territory with their sharp claws and **hard** beaks.

"**Owww!**" yelped Guff, as one of her crows pecked her on the forehead.

"At least look at us when you're talking, you insolent young pirate,"

squawked the crow.

"Sorry," apologised Guff, rubbing her head.

"Now, what do you want?"

said the crow, who was called William.

"Urm, well, I was just wondering.

OW!"

Guff screamed, as William the crow nutted her again.

"Out with it, pirate,"

shrieked William.

"Well I was just wondering,"

said Guff, looking into William's beady yellow eyes,

"would it be possible for you to vacate this nest for about **five minutes** while I come in and raise my flag?"

The **three** crows quickly huddled together and covered themselves with their wings.

Guff stole a glance at the other masts. It looked as though Wee Gladys was overcoming her crows and even old Fillet of Fish Fred appeared to be preparing to raise his flag.

"Certainly not! We've got traditions to uphold," said William.

"How would it look if we didn't try to peck you to death?"

William nodded towards Guff's cooking knife that hung from her belt.

"**Well,** I was just thinking, if you **did** allow me just **five minutes** of your time, then I'd quite happily allow you to use ...

... my own nest on board our ship if you needed a holiday, or fancied a change of scene, or whatever?"

Guff looked anxiously around as Barney Whiskers **stabbed** at the remaining crows in his nest.

There were feathers everywhere, as more and more crows flew into the air and away from the aggressive pirates.

"Hmm, let me discuss it with my fellows," said William, before going into another huddle of shiny black and blue wings.

"What's going on up there, Hairy Mole? I haven't seen her slash or swathe one jot!" squeaked Mr Bogey.

"Hang on a sec'!"

"Woooooooooooo!"

The crew **cheered** and **hollered** as suddenly the **Littleton** pirate flag appeared, **fluttering** in the breeze high above **Kettle Island Arena**.

"There she is," shouted Hairy Mole, as Guff looked out over the edge of her nest and waved to the crowd.

"Remember, it's only for a few minutes and then we're taking it down," squawked William.

"Quite right," said Guff, quickly clambering out of the nest and sliding down the mast.

"And if you need a holiday, you know where to come," Guff called out, as she slid down and rang the bell at the foot of the mast.

Ding a ling a ling a ling a ling!

"For she's a jolly good Guff, for she's a jolly good Guff, for she's a jolly good Guuuuuuuuuff and nobody can deny! HURRAH!"

everybody cheered.

Ding a ling a ling a ling a ling!

The sound of Wee Gladys the Mad's bell rang as she slid to the bottom of her mast and wiped feathers from her knife.

"GGGGGGGrrrrrrrrrrwelldone!"

growled Wee Gladys the Mad to Guff.

"Urm, thanks," said Guff with a beaming smile.

Then Barney Whiskers' bell sounded, ensuring that The Whiskers Gang came in third place.

Crevice and Pit cheered and high-fived as Guff ran back to the stands.

"That was amazing!" Guff laughed, as she got back to her seat.

"You were amazing!" smiled Hairy Mole. "Let me get you a celebratory something to say **well done!**"

Hairy Mole leapt to his feet and bounded down the wooden arena steps in search of a celebratory something for Guff.

Outside the arena, everyone was milling about and **growling** at each other, as they tried to get more grog or pickle-dogs before the next event at **four o'clock sharpish**.

Hairy Mole decided on a veggie rice and peas stand, and was *almost* at the front of the queue when he felt a tug at his arm.

At his hip there was a small boy.

"Are you Hairy Foal the Pirate?" asked the boy.

"It's **Mole** actually," sighed Hairy Mole. "What do you want, urchin?"

The small boy placed a piece of paper in Hairy Mole's hand, then skipped off in the direction of a Dunkin' Turnips stall.

"How peculiar!" said Hairy, looking down at the crumpled piece of paper in his hand.

Just then, out of the corner of his eye, Hairy Mole caught sight of a flash of black hair and a suggestion of red petticoats that disappeared as soon as he'd spotted them.

"Even stranger," he said to himself, as he reached the front of the veggie rice and peas queue and ordered Guff's celebratory something.

Nine

Puuuuuuuuuuull!

Inside **Kettle Island Arena,** Crevice and Pit were sitting quietly in the stands as they waited for their **Tug o' War** match against Billy and Barry Whiskers of **The Whiskers Gang.**

Hairy Mole gave Guff her celebratory veggie rice and peas and sat down next to Crevice and Pit.

"Ready Crevice? Ready Pit?" smiled Hairy Mole, as he handed a piece of paper to Crevice.

Down in the arena the first **Tug o' War** bout was taking place. Pirate Ken and Pirate Fred, from **The Pirate Pensioners,** were pulling against Fingers McGooly and Short-hand Phyllis from **The Daisy Headhunters.**

"Come on then, you little sausage rolls," shouted Pirate Ken, as he began to pull on the rope.

"Give it up, old pirate, your bones won't stand the beatin'," Short-hand Phyllis called back, as her partner Fingers McGooly dug his feet **deep** into the soft ground.

The Pirate Pensioners **pulled** and **pulled**, but there was no budging Fingers McGooly and Short-hand Phyllis.

"You'll have to do better than that, biscuit eaters!" laughed Fingers McGooly, as he began to feel the rope move in the pensioners' direction.

"Turnip botherers!!" screamed Pirate Fred, who **pulled** even harder.

The crowd were going wild and it was all that Wee Gladys the Mad could do to contain herself.

"COME ON, PUUUUULL!" she screamed from the stands.

Suddenly **The Daisy Headhunters** crouched their little legs and began to **pull** at an even lower angle.

The Pirate Pensioners flew through the air and **landed in the mud**.

"**Headhunters** Win!" shouted Wee Gladys.

In the stands Crevice and Pit were getting ready to meet the Whiskers boys.

"Now remember what I told you!"

Hairy Mole said, gulping as he saw Barry and Billy Whiskers punching each other for fun.

But it was too late for any more pep talk, as Crevice and Pit walked bravely to the centre of the arena to join the terrible twosome from **The Whiskers Gang**.

Crevice and Pit silently picked up the rope with their big hands and waited for the whistle.

"THREE!"

The twins steadied themselves.

"TWO!"

The Whiskers brothers growled and snarled.

"ONE!"

"Peeeeeeeeeeeeeep!"

All four pirates began to **pull**.

Barry and Billy quickly gathered the rope

and although Pit's grip was strong, his little feet couldn't hold on and he began to **slide** through the mud.

Crevice dug in firmly, but pretty soon he fell onto his bottom and found himself being **dragged** along the muddy ground.

"EASY! EASY!"

shouted **The Whiskers Gang** from the stands.

Crevice *just* managed to stop the slide and calmly remembered what was written on the crumpled piece of paper in his pocket.

"Knock, Knock!" Crevice shouted, much to Pit's surprise.

"What are you doing?" whispered Pit, thinking that his brother had gone mad.

But suddenly, Barry and Billy **stopped** pulling the rope.

"Who's there?" Billy asked curiously.

Figs," shouted Crevice.

"Figs who?"

"Figs your doorbell, as it seems to be broken!" Crevice shouted, and grabbed at the extra slack as the Whiskers boys slightly loosened their grip on the rope.

Pit looked on in amazement as the Whiskers boys began to chuckle.

"Say another," he shouted to Crevice.

"Knock, Knock!" Crevice yelled above the cheers of the crowd.

Billy Whiskers tried his best not to listen by biting his lip, but his brother couldn't resist answering.

"Who's there?" asked Barry.

"Gorilla!"

"No, Barry!"

But it was too late.

"Gorilla who?" asked Barry, unable to stop himself.

"Gorilla me a cheesy sandwich, 'coz I'm really hungry!"

"HAAAAAAAAAAAAA!" roared Barry and Billy, taking their big hands off the rope as they creased up in hoots of laughter.

"One more should do it!" shouted Pit.

"Knock, Knock!"

"Please stop!" said Barry. "Who's there?"

"Cash."

"Arrrgghhh! Nooooooo! Cash who?"

"Do you want a tissue for that cold? You sound terrible!"

"OOOOOOOWWWWW!"

The Whiskers boys let go of the rope completely and fell to the ground in peals of laughter.

"Yaaaaay," shouted Crevice and Pit, as they high-fived their big hands together in victory.

High in the stands the Littleton pirates cheered and waved, as they watched their shipmates happily slapping their hands together.

"That puts the twins into the *final* against The Daisy Headhunters!"

shouted Guff, as she watched Captain Whiskers *whacking* Barry and Billy around the head and *kicking* their big behinds out of the arena.

"If the twins win the **gold medal**, that means we'll be within a butterfly's wings of winning the **Pirate Olympic Cup!**" shouted Pickle.

"And then I won't have to win the hundred metres,"

whispered Hairy Mole to himself.

Ten

Official shenanigans

Sitting comfortably in their seats, Hairy Mole and his crew got ready for the final of the Tug o' War.

With Guff 's **gold medal** win in the Crow's Nest event, they were out in front on the medals table. If the twins could win the Tug o' War final, then they would be almost guaranteed the **Pirate Olympic Cup**.

But then Guff nudged Hairy Mole in the ribs and stopped his little daydream. She pointed to the centre of the arena, where there was some kind of Official Commotion going on.

Captain Bill Whiskers and his sons Billy and Barry had surrounded the judge and were being ten kinds of **horrible** to him, and **demanding** he disqualify Crevice and Pit for cheating.

The crowd waited for the judge to make an announcement. He picked up his megaphone and placed it to his lips.

"Ladies and gentlemen, boys and girls and, of course, pirates,"

the judge began, as Bill Whiskers poked him in the ribs with a **bony** finger.

"**After an official inquiry,**" the judge continued, "**it has been decided that The Littleton Pirates** CHEATED **in the Tug o' War by telling jokes!**"

Bill Whiskers **growled** a horrible laugh.

"Therefore they have been DISQUALIFIED and the scores for this year are as follows:

Gold to The Daisy Headhunters and **joint Silver** to The Pirate Pensioners and The Whiskers Gang!"

The crowd **gasped** and Hairy Mole hurried down from the stands to look at the **large** medals poster that was being put up at the entrance to the **Kettle Island Arena**.

Hairy Mole stared at the poster in **horror**. He knew there was now only **one way** that Littleton could win the
Pirate Olympic Cup.

That was if he could **win** the One Hundred Metre Pirate Bucket Boot race and The Daisy Headhunters would have to come in last place.

He *slowly* made his way back into the arena and started shining his **massive** pirate bucket boots, paying particular attention to the buckles, just in case a **certain someone** was watching from the stands.

MEDALS TABLE

1st place
The Daisy Headhunters
2 x Bronze and 1 x Silver and 2 x Gold – 10 points

2nd place
The Whiskers Gang
1 x Gold and 2 x Silver and 1 x Bronze – 8 points

2nd place
The Littleton Pirates
2 x Silver 1 x Bronze and 1 x Gold – 8 points

4th place
The Pirate Pensioners
1 x Gold and 1 Silver – 5 points

Sponsored by Badger's Burp Brewery

After a bit of a **stretch** and an extra **bottom scratch** for luck, Hairy Mole **pulled** on the huge boots and waded over to the starting line for the race of his life.

Eleven

Go on, Hairy Mole!

Hairy Mole stood alone at the start of the One Hundred Metre Pirate Bucket Boot track in the centre of **Kettle Island Arena.**

He felt as nervous as a skittle on a bowling lane, and did some more **stretches** just to take his mind off the race.

"Everyone's counting on me,"

Hairy Mole thought.

"All the people in Littleton, all my friends, all my family and all of the crew."

He looked to the crowd, where the rest of the crew were waving **Littleton** flags and calling out his name.

"Hairy,

Hairy,

Hairy!" they chanted.

Hairy Mole sucked in his more-than-ample tummy and puffed out his barrel-shaped chest, before trying to bend his legs (which, in oversized pirate bucket boots, can be a little bit tricky).

"Come on Mole, you can do it," he whispered to himself, as he (sort of) managed to touch the ground.

Hairy Mole looked across at the snarling faces of

Grandfather Mike from **The Pirate Pensioners,**

Tiny Tina from **The Daisy Headhunters**

and finally, in the fourth lane,

Captain Bill Whiskers.

All of the competitors' pirate bucket boots were well-polished and Hairy Mole did his best to ignore the strange squeaking sounds as his opponents limbered up and **stretched** in readiness for the final event.

An official walked over to the bell at the beginning of the hundred metre track and prepared to signal the start of the race.

"Come on, Hairy Mole," said the Mole sisters, as they watched on the TV in Bulbous Mole's front room.

"Run as fast as you can, Hairy Mole,"

said Smudge and Sparkle, as they listened on the radio in Sparkle's parents' kitchen.

"You can do it, Hairy Mole,"

said The Littleton Pirates, high up in the stands of Kettle Island Arena.

The four pirates started to run.

"Oi, wait for the bell,"

said the official, as he watched the pirates running off.

Ding a ling a ling a ling!

"GO HAIRY GO!" sang Mr Bogey and the rest of the crew.

Hairy Mole ran as fast as he could in the **massive** boots, and managed to gain an early lead.

"GO ONNNNNNNN!"
screamed the crew.

Hairy Mole could feel the wind on his face as he **ran** and **ran** as fast as he could.

But suddenly **good** wind turned to bad, as he smelled the **foul breath** of Captain Whiskers on his shoulder and he could hear the approaching **stamp** of Grandfather Mike from The Pirate Pensioners.

"You can do it," Hairy Mole said under his breath, just as he noticed Grandfather Mike beginning to overtake him.

"WOW! Look at that pensioner go!"
shouted Pickle.

"Must have heard there's a sale on Jaffa cakes," said Guff quietly.

Just behind Hairy Mole, Tiny Tina from **The Daisy Headhunters** was catching him up.

At the 50 metres stage it was Hairy Mole, Captain Whiskers and Grandfather Mike neck and neck and neck,

but just when Hairy Mole started to pull away, Captain Whiskers elbowed him in the ribs and got in front.

"Go on, Captain," snarled **The Whiskers Gang** from the stands.

"GO ON HAIRY!" yelled Guff and Pickle, as they watched their captain fall behind Bill Whiskers and Grandfather Mike.

"Speed it up now, Grandfather," shouted **The Pirate Pensioners** from underneath their tartan rugs.

It was anyone's race with twenty metres to go, with **The Whiskers Gang** in first place,

The Pensioners second

and **Littleton** third.

"Come on, Skipper," squeaked Mr Bogey at the top of his Squeaky voice, as Hairy Mole edged closer to the finishing line.

Ten metres from the line, Tiny Tina from **The Daisy Headhunters** caught up with the others and ran level with

Hairy Mole,
Grandfather Mike and
Bill Whiskers,

making it neck and neck and neck and neck.

"Go Tina go! Go Tina go!"
shouted **The Daisy Headhunters**, as they jumped up and down like goats in a cactus field.

"Come on Hairy Mole!" screamed

110

Guff, as she climbed on to the twins' shoulders to get a better view.

Hairy Mole ran as **fast** as he could, and with five metres left to go he stepped ahead of Grandfather Mike and past Tiny Tina.

But he couldn't catch Bill Whiskers – until suddenly ...

"Paaaaaaaaaarrrrp!"

There was a noise like **thunder** that ripped through the screams and shouts of the crowd.

It sounded like a **large** ship approaching, and there were quite a few pirates who turned to see if they could see any **funnels** appearing in the distance.

Hairy Mole, on the other hand, had no time to stop and catch his thoughts or anything else for that matter,
as he was **propelled** forward by
the *intense* pressure shooting out from his bottom.

He **flew** like a cannonball,

   past Grandfather Mike,

   past Tiny Tina,

   past Captain Whiskers

and on until finally **he ran out of gas**, just as he tumbled over the finishing line in **first place**.

"Yaaaaaaaaaaay," shouted the crew.

"Wooooooooooooo!" whooped the whole arena, as they watched the **brave** smelly-bottomed pirate lying on the floor holding his **burning behind**.

"Yaaaaaaaaaaay!" shouted The Daisy Headhunters, as Tiny Tina crossed the line in **third place**.

As the crew gathered around him, Hairy Mole looked up at their smiling faces and whimpered, "What happened?"

"You won, Captain, you won!" yelled Guff.

"What about **The Daisy Headhunters?**" asked Hairy Mole, looking across –   – to the finishing line.

"They came in third place!" squeaked Mr Bogey.

"So what does that mean?"

"It means," said a snarling Wee Gladys the Mad (she may have been smiling) "that we share the Pirate Olympic Cup. Right?"

"Right you are Gladys, sounds good to me!" smiled Hairy Mole, as he looked at his crew happily nodding and shaking hands with The Daisy Headhunters.

"And?" began Hairy Mole.

"WHAT?" shouted everybody.

"Urm, what happened to my bottom?" said Hairy Mole, with reddening cheeks.

"Let's just say that all those extra helpings of cabbage soup must have paid off!" squeaked Mr Bogey.

The crew lifted Hairy Mole high above their heads and danced around Kettle Island Arena, singing and dancing like ferrets in a fire engine. "Hip Hip Hooray!" "Hip Hip Hooray!"

Twelve

Celebrate good times

That evening, under the light of Kettle Island moon, a **huge feast** marked the end of the **one hundred and first Pirate Olympic Games.**

In the centre of **Kettle Island Arena,** a gigantic table covered in:

pickles, turnips, mongers, cheese, jam and grog had been laid out for all the pirate competitors and officials.

It was a splendid sight, and wherever you looked pirates of all **shapes** and sizes were busily **scoffing** down food and washing down grog as if they'd been at sea for **longer than a leech on licorice.**

After the meal, the Mayor of Kettle Island rang a little bell and cleared his throat in readiness for a speech.

Ding a ling a ling a ling!

"Order, order," an official shouted.

"Dear pirates, thank you all f ...

... Aaaaagggrrrrgghhhh"

screamed the mayor,
as he was **grabbed** from behind and passed along the table by more **rough and ready** pirate hands than sail on the Spanish Main.

In all the commotion, Wee Gladys the Mad leapt onto the table and grabbed the **Pirate Olympic Cup** in between her tiny hands.

116

"I think," she began with a snarl, "what his Mayorness is trying to say is: The Headhunters and The Littleton Pirates have won the Pirate Olympic Cup. So, let's have a party!"

"Arrrrrrrrrrrrrrrrrrrr!"

yelled all the pirates in agreement.

"This is the best day ever," shouted Guff, as she jumped around like a newborn nipper hog.

"You can say that again, Guffer," squeaked Mr Bogey, as he joined her in a jig.

Hairy Mole was having a brilliant time and had forgotten all about his **burning bottom** as he danced with Wee Gladys the Mad, making sure not to swing her round too much for fear of upsetting her current 'caring and sharing' mood.

"So then, Mole, who gets to keep the cup?" **growled** Gladys, as Captain Fothergill's Band stopped playing for a grog break.

"**Urm**," Hairy began, "how about **we** keep it for **six months** and then **you** can have it for **six months**?"

Wee Gladys thought for a moment as they walked to the edge of the dance floor.

"How about **we** 'av it for **12 months** and I don't cut your legs off?" she snapped.

"**Ahahaha!**" laughed Hairy Mole before he saw the look on Gladys' face.

She looked **as stern as a mule** and **as angry as a parrot**, and Hairy Mole gulped as she edged forwards.

118

"I'm only joking with you, you fat old pirate!"

and Gladys laughed with a cackle that sent goosebumps chasing shivers down Hairy Mole's more than adequate spine.

"Good one, Gladys," laughed Hairy Mole, wiping a bead of sweat from his brow.

"Good one."

"We'll 'av it first and then you can 'av it!"

shouted Gladys.

"Yes, agreed, and quite right too," smiled Hairy Mole as he shook hands with the tiny captain.

Hairy Mole was still smiling as he sat down on a bench by the edge of the dance floor, but he quickly stopped as he felt a **rough** hand on his shoulder.

He turned around to see the ugly face of Bill Whiskers staring down at him.

"You haven't heard the last of us, Hairy Fool!" growled Captain Whiskers.

"Yeah!" growled the rest of The Whiskers Gang, who were just behind him.

And with that, Captain Bill Whiskers and his gang of troublemakers stomped off back to their ship with **extremely angry faces** and **very stern frowns** indeed.

Hairy Mole watched as they disappeared out of sight. He thought he caught a glimpse of Pirate Betsy's red scarlet dress flicking past a Dunkin' Turnips stall, but it could have been just the sunset playing tricks on his eyes.

She didn't even turn to wave goodbye.

Hairy felt slightly sad as Mr Bogey sat down next to him.

"All OK, Skipper?" squeaked Mr Bogey.

"Yes Bogey, I'm fine thank you," said Hairy Mole quietly.

Just then, Hairy Mole felt a tug on his sleeve.

"Oi there, pirate. I've got something for you, if you've got a brass piece for me."

A dirty urchin smiled up at Hairy Mole and grinned a toothy grin.

Hairy Mole placed a **brass piece** into the whippersnapper's hand and was promptly handed a crumpled piece of paper.

The urchin disappeared into the crowd as Hairy Mole unfolded the piece of paper.

Well done Hairy Mole.
Until we meet again.
Pirate Betsy xxx

Hairy Mole's cheeks began to redden and his heart skipped a beat, as he shoved the piece of paper into the pocket of his pirate waistcoat.

"Happy days eh, Hairy Mole?" squeaked Mr Bogey.

"Happy days indeed, Mr Bogey. Happy days indeed!" he grinned.

Thirteen

At home with T-towel

Back home in **Littleton-on-Sea**, T-towel the cat cleaned her whiskers and listened to the sounds of celebration coming through the open window in the front room.

T-towel wasn't fond of festivities or noise, but even she had managed to enjoy the sight of Bulbous Mole and her sister Humongous leaping about like mountain goats on pogo-sticks, as Hairy Mole had guffed his way to **gold** in the **Pirate Olympics.**

"Who'd have thought it?" T-towel smiled to herself, before turning round three times to find a more **comfortable** position on her more than **comfortable** cushion.

*"Hairy Mole's **bottom** has actually helped him to win something other than worn pantaloons and a smell that could peel cabbages."*

With this thought in her mind, T-towel closed her little eyes and dreamed of butterflies on toast as the cheers, songs and laughter from Littleton-on-Sea continued to drift through the open window – until finally she fell into a **deep** and **extremely contented sleep**.

The End

The End